MW00942643

The Trespassers Club

Helen Vivienne Fletcher

First published by HVF Publishing in 2018

Copyright © Helen Vivienne Fletcher, 2018

All rights reserved. No part of this publication may be reproduced, stored, or transmitted in any form or by any means, electronic, mechanical, photocopying, recording, scanning, or otherwise without written permission from the publisher.

It is illegal to copy this book, post it to a website, or distribute it by any other means without permission.

Cover design by Ian and Alana Garmonsway.

This hardcover edition first published in 2021.

ISBN:
978-0-473-58443-6 (hardcover)
978-0-473-58444-3 (hardcover – POD)
978-0-473-45690-0 (paperback)
978-0-473-45692-4 (mobi)
978-0-473-45691-7 (epub)

DEDICATION

For my sister, Julia, and her son, Mahe.

CHAPTER ONE

We crouched low to the ground. I shuffled forward and signalled to the others that it was safe to move on. No-one had seen us yet, but we were in danger of being spotted.

Behind me one of my team yawned then stifled a giggle. I frowned and crouched lower in case our enemies had heard. We couldn't risk getting caught now.

We heard a shout; our names called. Someone was on to us, we had to hurry or … Behind me the giggling grew louder. Didn't they realise how important this was? The whole mission depended on our not being seen.

I froze as a flicker of moving cloth caught my eye. A woman carrying a washing basket appeared to my right. I dropped lower to the ground. She came closer but didn't see me. I was sure she must be able to hear me breathing.

She picked up a red beach towel and pegged it to the line. Perhaps this was a signal to her spies? I glanced around, trying to spot any other targets.

My team shuffled forward while her back was turned. Mud squelched up between my bare toes. I wrinkled my nose but kept quiet.

I heard a whisper behind me. It was my sister, Katy.

"Why did we agree to play this stupid game?"

"Oh, come on. It's fun." That was Amy. "Anyway, we'll probably never have to do it again."

The woman at the washing line looked up, and the conversation stopped. She had just started pegging again when:

"Laura? Katy?"

The shout caught me by surprise. I toppled over into the grass. Katy and the other girls fell down beside me, laughing. The woman jumped, then laughed too as she recognised us.

"Trespassing again, are you?" she asked.

"Last meeting of the Trespassers Club, Mrs Taylor," I said.

Last meeting, I thought to myself.

CHAPTER TWO

"There you are." My mother appeared above us. "What's so funny?"

"Nothing Mum." Katy rolled her eyes and gave an irritated huff. We pulled ourselves up and stood staring at each other.

Mum gave Mrs Taylor a smile, then ushered us out of her garden.

"We're just about ready to leave," Mum said. "You should say your goodbyes now." She turned and walked back towards the house.

I didn't look at the other girls. I didn't want them to see how upset I was.

Amy rubbed my arm. "It's okay, Laura. We can e-mail each other." She flicked her long, red plait over her shoulder, but it whacked my chest, bouncing back. "Oops, sorry!" She giggled, covering her mouth.

I looked away, blinking. Amy was by far the nicest of our neighbours, and I hated the idea of not seeing her every day.

Hannah gave Katy a hug. "And we'll still see you at school, Katy."

Katy noticed me watching and pushed me away. "Get lost, Laura," she snapped. "They are my friends, not yours."

"But …"

"I said, GET LOST!"

I looked at Amy and Hannah. Amy stared at her feet and Hannah tried to hide a smirk.

I turned away. My stomach hurt, but I didn't think Katy would care. I swallowed and walked towards the car.

"You shouldn't be so hard on her, Katy," Amy said quietly.

I looked back, but Hannah's cloud of frizzy hair blocked Amy and Katy's faces from view.

"It's not my fault she doesn't have any friends." Katy didn't bother to lower her voice.

I started to run.

Mum and Dad had the car all packed up ready to go. Mum stood beside it, ruffling her hair up into a half ponytail. She looked worried and I could tell she thought she'd forgotten something.

I put my shoes on and climbed into the back seat. The car had been sitting in the sun, causing everything to heat up. It was already boiling inside, and we hadn't even started driving yet. I put my water bottle in the seat pocket in front of me and fished my book out of my bag.

"I've told you before: don't read while we're driving. It'll make you sick," Mum said.

I made a face at the book and opened it anyway. I watched over the top of it as Dad cleaned his glasses on his sleeve. He looked funny without them, like a mole, the way he peered short-sightedly at everything. Katy looked like him. Not the short-sighted part but she had the same soft, round face and features. I looked more like Mum, all sharp angles and cheekbones.

Katy walked back to the car with a scowl on her face. She flopped down on the seat next to me and took out her phone.

"Hey, Katy, do you want to …" I stopped as Katy glared at me. She put on her headphones and turned away. Dad gave me a little smile and shrugged.

My head started to ache almost straight away, but I didn't want to admit it to Mum. I put the book down and reached forward to get my water bottle.

Katy slapped my back. I gasped. My skin stung where she'd hit me. I turned and glared at her. She stared out the window with a stupid smile on her face, like she hadn't done anything. I flopped back in the seat and closed my eyes. *Ignore her*, I thought, *just ignore her.*

"What you gonna do, Laura?" Katy leaned right

over me to whisper, and I felt her breath on my cheek.

I opened my eyes, ready to yell at her, but she kicked my ankle before I could.

"Ow!" I yelped.

It wasn't even a gentle kick, she did it with the heel of her shoe, so it really hurt. She grinned at me and waited to see what I'd do. Something seemed to bunch up inside me like a spring being pushed down. I punched her shoulder as hard as I could.

Katy's mouth pinched up into a tight line. "Mum! Laura punched me!"

"Laura!" Mum twisted round in her seat to glare at me. "You are too old for that kind of behaviour."

"Katy's older than me and she started it!" My voice made a horrible whiny sound.

"I don't care who started it! Just behave."

I felt like I was going to cry. Katy pushed out her bottom lip and made blubbing noises. Ugh! And to think I'd been worried that Katy wouldn't want to play with me anymore. Who'd want to play with a bully like her! I closed my book and stuck it in the seat pocket in front of me. It was too hot to read anyway. I settled back in my seat, determined to ignore Katy for the rest of the journey.

CHAPTER THREE

I must have fallen asleep. When I woke up, we were at the new house. Mum shook my shoulder. "Come on, sweetie. Wake up now."

I looked around. "Where's Katy?" I asked.

"She's already inside."

That was just like her not to wait for me. I got out of the car and walked up the stairs to the house, but when I reached the fence I noticed something. I stopped and peered at it.

"Mum, look!" I pointed to some blue squiggles drawn on the white palings.

Mum clicked her tongue. "Tagging. We'll have to clean that off in the morning."

"Why?" I tried to read the tags, but the spray-painted letters overlapped, making them hard to decipher.

"For one thing, it looks untidy, and we don't want to encourage more of it. After all, some people find it intimidating."

I glanced up at Mum. "Intimidating? How come?"

Mum frowned. "Well, if someone drew all over your bedroom walls, you'd feel like they'd invaded your personal space. It can make people feel like their homes aren't safe anymore."

I nodded slowly, trying to understand.

"Come on, let's get inside."

I followed Mum up the stairs, into the house. I liked the big spaces filled only with boxes. Already I was imagining games we could play around them. In my head they were relics from a past age. I felt like an explorer searching for my lost sister.

"Katy? Katy, where are you?" I called.

"Boo!" Katy jumped out from behind one of the boxes.

I screamed, and she fell about laughing as I glared at her. I felt my shoulders rising up unevenly and I bit my lip. Why did she keep doing that? I didn't think it was funny.

"Do you want to play a game or something?" I asked.

"No." She hesitated for a moment, looking at me. "But we'll play tomorrow, okay?"

CHAPTER FOUR

In the morning, I was the last to get up. I hadn't slept well but I was eager to get outside and start exploring the neighbourhood. As soon as I walked into the kitchen, I could tell Katy was in a grump.

"There's no milk." She snapped the words out, as if it were my fault.

I made a face, screwing up my mouth and nose. "There's no milk," I mimicked her in my most annoying whiny voice.

Her eyes narrowed, and I shrank back against the wall. For a moment it looked like she was going to throw a tantrum, then she tossed her hair and gave an exaggerated sigh.

"Stop standing like that, it grosses me out," she said.

I looked down at my feet. My toes were pointing inwards. I twisted them out into ballet position.

Katy glared at me. "Don't do that with your ribs either. It's yuck."

I shook my head and looked away. Lately, I'd developed a habit of standing with my ribs pushed out to the left. It did look a little weird, like my body was broken, but for some reason it really annoyed Katy.

"Leave her alone Katy." Dad walked past Katy's chair and gently pulled one of the straggly bits of blonde hair that had crept out of her plait. If I'd done that she probably would have hit me. Instead, she was trying to stop a smile from forcing its way through her scowl.

I popped a couple of pieces of bread in the toaster.

"Make me some too," Katy said.

"*Please,*" I muttered. I put the toast on a plate and handed it to Katy. "What time do you want to play?" I asked.

Katy frowned. "I don't want to. Go away."

"But you promised!" My voice had gone all whiny again.

"Maybe I will in a couple of weeks."

"But the school holidays will be over in a couple of weeks. Please!"

"No!"

Dad looked up from the paper. "Oh, go on Katy," he said. "Be nice to your sister."

Katy looked like she was going to argue then she rolled her eyes. "Okay, okay. We'll play when we've finished breakfast."

"Can you make it an outside game?" Dad asked. "Your mum and I have got to start unpacking in here."

I nodded. That suited me just fine.

CHAPTER FIVE

"What do you want to play?"

I think Katy knew my answer even before it left my mouth. "Trespassers Club," I said.

There was an old, broken-down fence running between our property and the empty section next door. We climbed through it, ducking down to stay hidden.

"Ow! Laura, help–"

I looked back just in time to see Katy tumble over, landing face down in the grass. "Are you okay?" I called. I couldn't help laughing as Katy struggled to right herself. Her plait had landed straight out from the top of her head like a handle, and I was tempted to give it a tug.

"My foot's stuck." Katy pulled herself free, then sat up, glaring at me. "You could have helped," she said.

I shrugged and gave her a hand getting to her feet. We looked around at the section. It was full of long grass, all the way up to our waists at some points. I stumbled through it, having to lift my legs up much higher than normal just to be able to walk.

"It's beautiful," I said. We'd found our own private field. Katy actually smiled at me.

Suddenly, I heard a dog growl and saw grass moving in the corner of the section.

Katy grabbed my hand. "Run!"

The dog became a beast that could melt us if we looked into its eyes. The overgrowth kept us safe, hiding the beast from us, but if it came too close we would be forced to look at it. We ran as fast as we could, beating our way through the grass.

"Come on, Laura. Faster!" Katy yanked my arm, knocking my feet from under me.

"I can't," I tried to say, but I was too out of breath.

We got to the other side of the section. A fence blocked our way.

"What do we do now?" I yelled. The beast was close behind us. We could hear it barking and growling.

"Climb the fence!"

Katy gave me a boost then climbed up herself. We dropped down on the other side. Katy started laughing.

I grabbed her arm. "Don't look back! The beast will melt you," I said.

Katy frowned. "What are you talking about?"

"The beast … it will melt you."

She glanced back, confused. "Laura, it's just a dog. A big scary one, but still just a dog."

I looked back. She was right. The dog growled at me and pawed the fence like it wanted to eat me, but it wasn't a beast, and it didn't melt me with its eyes. I felt my stomach drop with disappointment.

"Sometimes you really are weird." Katy got up and dusted herself off. "Come on. Let's go down to the street."

CHAPTER SIX

"Hey, Laura, come look at this." Katy stood, staring through some trees.

I peered in between the branches. At the back of a large untidy section was the oldest house I had ever seen.

"I think it's abandoned," Katy said. "It looks like it, don't you think?"

I nodded. The house looked like it had been empty for years. There were trees almost all the way around except for a gap where there must once have been a path.

We stared through at the garden. The grass was almost as high as in the empty lot, and the paint was peeling off the house. It had two symmetrical windows, one of which was smashed, so it looked like the house was winking. It was so broken down I couldn't see it as a real building – it looked more like a Wendy-house at the bottom of an unkempt garden.

"Let's go inside." Katy's eyes sparkled.

I felt my toes turning in again. "Why don't we just keep playing Trespassers Club?" I said.

"This is just like Trespassers Club. We just go inside the house instead of in the garden." Katy made it sound so simple. "Do you think we could get in through that window?" she asked.

I looked at the small window. It was too high up for a start.

Katy started off towards the house. "Come on, let's try." She took off, then squealed as she reached the grass. "Careful, Laura, it's really slushy."

I followed after her, only because I couldn't think of an excuse not to. My feet slipped and sunk into the mud, sliding about so much it was hard to keep going. Katy got further and further away from me.

"Hurry up! You're taking ages," she called back over her shoulder. She was nearly at the house. I did my best to run and catch up with her.

When we got to the door, Katy went to knock but it swung open. The lock had been forced.

"Someone must have broken in." Katy seemed excited.

I gulped at the thought we might walk in on someone.

Suddenly we heard noises coming from inside.

Squeeeak … Thump … Thump … Squeeeak … Thump … Thump …

Katy and I froze. Someone was inside. My chest hurt, and my palms were sweating. I tried to swallow but it felt like my throat was clogged up with play dough. Katy squeezed my arm. I could tell we were thinking the same thing. We had to run!

I don't know what made me do it. My head was thinking run, but suddenly my legs were moving forward. I went into the house, leaving Katy on the doorstep.

CHAPTER SEVEN

I followed the noise into what must have been a bedroom. My head pounded from holding my breath, and my legs felt like they'd been replaced with marshmallow. Everything was still for a second.

A shape hurtled through the window. I screamed and threw my hands over my face.

"Laura! Laura!" Katy ran into the room.

"It's okay! It's okay," I said. "It's just a cat."

Katy's eyes were wide, and her face pale.

"Look." I pointed to the fluffy black and white cat, which had sprung back out the window when I screamed. We stayed still and quiet, until it climbed in the window again and jumped to land on a set of bunk-beds. The mattress springs squeaked, like they were complaining about the cat's weight, then there was a thump as the top bunk hit the wall.

"I thought …" Katy sighed and shook her head. "Just don't scare me like that, okay?"

We looked around. The room was full of furniture and the wardrobe had clothes in it too, but everything was grey and dusty. It was like someone had gone out for the day and just never come home again.

"Isn't it strange how everything's been left here?" I said.

In the living room we found a television and there were even pictures on the walls – family photos of very serious looking people. Someone had drawn a moustache on the face of one of the women.

I looked at Katy, my stomach dropping. "Katy, what if this isn't an abandoned house? Maybe it's just been broken into and that's why the door was open."

"Don't be silly. Look how old everything is. They don't even make TVs like that anymore." Katy flicked the light switch. "See? No power."

"But why would someone leave all their stuff behind? It doesn't make sense."

Katy shrugged then started to smile. "Actually … Oh, no, I'm not supposed to tell you."

I frowned. "Tell me what?"

"No, no, I can't tell you. You'll just get scared."

"No, I won't."

Katy shook her head.

"Aw, please Katy."

Katy tipped her head to the side, studying me. "Do you promise not to tell anyone?"

I nodded.

"Okay." Katy narrowed her eyes and lowered her voice. "There was a little boy who lived here. He was about your age, then one day he just disappeared. His parents left the house and searched the whole country looking for him, but they never saw him again."

I felt my chest growing tight. The back of my neck started to tingle. "Stop trying to scare me," I said.

"I'm not trying to scare you. It's true."

I swallowed. "What happened to him?"

Katy smiled. She lowered her voice and leaned in close to me. "They think someone kidnapped him. Apparently lots of kids that age go missing in this neighbourhood. In fact, they think this is where the kidnappers hang out. They wait until the kids come right inside the house and then–"

Something brushed up against my leg. My breath caught in my throat. I closed my eyes and screamed.

CHAPTER EIGHT

Katy fell about laughing. I looked down and saw the cat winding itself around my legs.

"That was really mean. I'm going to tell Mum," I said.

Katy groaned. "Oh, grow up. It was funny!" She kicked the floor. "Come on, let's go. This place is such a dump."

Katy turned back when I didn't follow. "Are you coming?" she snapped.

I hesitated. "What about the cat?" I said. "It might have been the boy's. Probably no-one's fed it in ages. We should find some food for it."

Katy shook her head. "You're such a baby, Laura!" She turned and ran off without me.

"Katy? Katy, wait!" I called, but she didn't even look back.

I wasn't sure if I was brave enough to stay in the house by myself. I looked back at the cat then trudged back through the muddy garden. My feet slipped and slid, the mud sucking and pulling at me, like … quicksand! I'd fallen into a patch of quicksand! I had to keep moving or I'd sink.

Something rustled in the trees and the hairs on the back of my neck rose up. I looked around. I had the creepy feeling I was being watched.

"Hello?" I called in a shaky voice.

No one answered, but I was sure someone was there. I swallowed and I kept walking. I heard the rustle again, then a flash of something moved behind the trees. I tried to run but my foot was stuck.

"Help! Katy!" I screamed. "I'm stuck! Please, somebody help!"

She didn't answer, probably already back at home. The rustling seemed to be coming from everywhere. I covered my face too scared to look.

"For goodness sake, Laura." Katy trudged back up the garden towards me. "It's just mud."

"But there was someone in the trees! And the quicksand–"

She pulled my shoe out of the mud. "Stop making things up," she said.

"I'm not. There really was someone there!" I looked back at the trees. I couldn't see anyone now, but I was sure they'd been there.

Katy shook her head and walked away. "Hurry up," she called over her shoulder. "I'm not waiting for you."

I rushed after Katy. I did not want to be left behind.

CHAPTER NINE

Katy was in a sulk that night at dinner. It started when Mum asked if we would help unpack the next day.

"Aw, Mum, do we have to?" Katy voice was horribly high-pitched and whiny. She sounded like a sick cat yowling.

"It would be a really big help if you did." Dad didn't look up from his food. "It won't take long."

"I don't want to. I've got better things to do." Katy flicked her hair over her shoulder and looked away. She started to mash her peas into a paste with her fork. Mum and Dad glanced at each other.

"We'd like you both to help." Mum's voice was firm.

"Why should we? It wasn't our idea to move," Katy snapped.

There was a silence, during which I was sure everyone could hear the food sticking in my throat.

"Katy …" Mum said eventually.

Katy got up and stormed off to her bedroom. Dad followed her. He shut the door, but Mum and I could still hear them yelling.

"Finish your dinner, love," Mum said. She tried to sound cheery, but it didn't work. I could tell she was upset.

I looked down at my food. My stomach shrunk as the yelling continued.

Mum frowned at me. "Well, if you're not going to eat it you can go to your room too."

"It's not my fault Katy's in a strop." I glared at Mum.

Mum's eyes went really wide then narrowed down to slits. "Don't you start, Laura."

"But I'm not!"

"I said go to your room Laura." Mum shook her head. She wasn't even listening to me.

I dropped my knife and fork onto the plate. They made a huge clattering noise which made me feel better. I stormed off to my room, just like Katy had.

CHAPTER TEN

"Please play with me, Katy." I pulled at Katy's arm.

She shook me off. "No, get lost."

"Pleeease. I've got no-one else to talk to."

Katy stared at me then smiled. "Okay, but I get to choose the game."

She chose hide and seek, so I hid in the airing cupboard. It was cramped and hot, and my knees were up round my face, but I didn't care. At least, I didn't care until half an hour had passed, and Katy still hadn't found me.

I climbed out and stumbled into the living room. My feet had gone to sleep, and pins and needles shot up my legs as I tried to walk.

Katy was sitting on the couch reading a magazine.

"Katy?"

She looked at me with a stupid smirk on her face. I turned and ran to my room.

"Laura, what's wrong?" Mum asked when she found me crying.

I shook my head. "Katy," I said.

Mum sighed. "You know, you don't have to play with your sister all the time. You could play by yourself."

I didn't look at Mum. She didn't know how hard it was to be lonely.

Over the next few days, Katy got even more moody. She kept storming out and slamming doors, then she started to go off by herself. I followed her one day and found that she was hanging out in the empty section next door. She'd lie in the grass for hours listening to her headphones and messaging her friends.

I decided maybe playing by myself wasn't such a bad idea, but playing Trespassers Club seemed silly with just one person. What I needed was a place of my own. Katy had the field; I needed somewhere too – somewhere where no-one was likely to go, especially Katy.

I needed the abandoned house.

CHAPTER ELEVEN

My bedroom window had seemed low enough to climb out of, but now I was trying it I wasn't so sure. I swung my leg out over the sill and got ready to jump.

"Laura? Laura, where are you?" Mum called.

I held my breath, hoping she wouldn't come into my room. I heard the kitchen door open and let the breath out in a rush. Thank goodness, she was going outside. I pulled my other leg over the edge of the sill and slid out.

My feet hit the ground, sending a jolt up my shins, and I tumbled forward onto my knees. Suddenly, I heard footsteps and Mum came around the side of the house.

I ducked under the fence and ran for it.

I crept through the neighbours' gardens, keeping out of sight of the windows. If I could get to the house from around the back, I wouldn't have to risk getting stuck in the mud again.

I flattened myself against the side of a house as a woman came outside. She dumped some big supermarket bags of rubbish into her bin, squashing them down. My head pounded from holding my breath, but finally she went back inside. I dropped to my knees, so she couldn't see me from the window, and crawled across her lawn.

The abandoned house's back garden was the fifth one along from our place. It was lower than the other gardens and I peered down into the overgrown trees and bushes. They were so thick, I could barely see through. I pushed through the first lot, but then tripped and skidded down a bank.

I got caught on some branches, which slowed my fall. I tried to stand up, but my shirt was stuck. When I pulled away the fabric tore, leaving a big gap near my belly button. Mum was going to be mad! I looked around and shivered as I stood up.

It was much darker in this garden than it had been in the others, making it colder too. Tall, twisted trees surrounded the edge of a slushy lawn, and boards poked out between them from the remains of an old fence. I found a blackberry bush and pulled at the berries.

"Ow!" I jerked my hand back, dropping the berries. There was purple berry blood on my fingers and a little bead of red on the end of my pinkie, where I'd caught it on a briar. I sucked on it then wandered around to the front of the house.

There was something moving around inside. I stopped on the doorstep, afraid to go in, the hairs on my arms rising into goosebumps. I took a breath. It was just the cat from before, I thought. Nothing more, just the cat.

I went in. My breath stuck in my throat, all my muscles tightened. There was somebody in the house.

CHAPTER TWELVE

He was a few years older than me. He eyed the door like he wanted to run, but I was blocking it. "Who are you?" he said eventually.

"Laura." My voice shook.

"Jacob." He gave a little nod of his head.

I swallowed, thinking of the story Katy had told me when we came to the house before. "Are you a kidnapper?" I asked.

His forehead creased up. "A kidnapper? No." He kept staring at me.

I wanted to stare back but I was too shy. Instead I snuck looks at him. He had big dark eyes and a floppy fringe, just like a Jersey cow. Suddenly, I was picturing a cow standing in front of me wearing clothes. I started giggling, and he frowned.

"I'm sorry … It's just … the cow …"

Jacob looked away.

I blushed, feeling silly for saying anything. "We just moved here," I said, after a while.

"I saw the van."

"Do you live around here?"

Jacob nodded, but he didn't give me a proper answer. I didn't know what else to ask him and I wondered if I should go. He didn't seem to want to talk to me.

"I didn't think anyone else knew about this place," I said.

Jacob shrugged. "Most of the kids around here do. Not many come here though. They think it's haunted."

I swallowed. "I'm not scared."

"You were the other day."

"You *were* following me!"

"I saw you get stuck in the mud. Is your sister always that angry?" Jacob smiled for the first time.

"She is at the moment. She's mad that we moved away from our old place."

Jacob nodded. "I moved last year. It's tough at first."

"We were playing Trespassers Club," I said. "You try to trespass in other people's gardens without being seen. It's fun and … stuff." My voice trailed off at the end of that. Jacob didn't seem very interested, and it felt stupid to keep talking. He tugged at the end of his shirt and didn't look up.

"Why's this place empty?" I asked, after a bit.

"My mum said the lady who lived here left it when she went into a rest home." Jacob shrugged. "Apparently, her son owns it now, but he lives in England, so he never visits."

I nodded. "It seems like a good place to hang out," I said.

"Maybe."

I picked at the dried blood on my pinkie, and Jacob stared at the ground between his feet. I swallowed, trying to think of something to say, but then Jacob glanced back at me.

"What were you saying about kidnappers?" he asked.

"Just something Katy said. It doesn't matter." I felt a blush creeping up my neck again. I kept talking to cover my embarrassment. "We didn't know there were any kids living around here. I'll have to tell Katy about you."

"No!" Jacob's eyes flashed and his lips pulled back over his teeth.

I stepped backwards. Jacob glared at me. His hands were clenching up into fists.

I swallowed and took a breath. "I have to go," I said. I headed for the door.

"Hey!" Jacob grabbed my arm. "Don't tell anyone I'm here. Okay?"

I nodded. He stared at me then let go of my arm. I ran for it.

CHAPTER THIRTEEN

I rushed through the neighbours' gardens, not bothering to stay hidden. I clambered over a fence and my fingernails bent back, ripping as they broke.

"Ow!" I let go of the fence and landed splat on the other side.

"It's okay," I said to myself. "You're safe." My words came out shaky though. I tried to take some deep breaths before sitting up.

A shadow fell over me. "Hello there."

I shrank back against the fence.

"It's okay, don't be frightened," said the voice.

I peered up at the speaker. She looked like a grandmother, her face covered in soft folds of skin that looked like they were stuffed with cotton wool.

She smiled at me, and her eyes twinkled.

"Hi," I said.

"You must be one of the girls who moved in next door."

"Yes, I'm Laura."

The lady smiled. "Hello, Laura. My name's Margaret." Margaret held out her hand, and I shook it. She helped me up, and I brushed myself off.

"Would you like to come in?" She made a tutting noise. "Looks like you've hurt your hand."

I looked down. My fingers were bleeding where the nails had bent back. I wrapped my hand in the end of my torn shirt.

Margaret chuckled. "Come on, I'll get you a Band-Aid."

I hesitated. Mum wouldn't like me going into a stranger's house, but then again, she was our neighbour, and she didn't seem very scary.

We went in the back door, through the kitchen and into the dining room. The room was crammed full of what Mum would call bric-a-brac. She had a whole wall covered in patterned china plates, and every surface held little ornaments. I couldn't help staring.

Margaret got some antiseptic and cleaned my fingernail. I squirmed as it stung.

Margaret smiled. "That's the worst of it." She wrapped a Band-Aid around the tip of my finger. "Now, would you like a biscuit, Laura?" Margaret offered me a plate of biscuits that looked homemade.

I took one. "Thank you."

"How old are you, dear?" Margaret asked.

"I turned ten last month."

"So I won't be teaching you."

"You're a teacher?" My eyes widened. She was so old!

"Yes, at the local High School." Margaret smiled.

"Greenvale High?"

"That's it."

"Katy's going there when term starts."

"Is she your sister?"

I nodded.

"It's a good school. There are few trouble makers who cause problems but nothing we can't handle."

"I hope Katy likes it."

"It must be nice for the two of you to have each other."

I shrugged, not sure how else to answer.

Margaret leaned in closer. "Or maybe not?"

"Katy's okay."

Margaret smiled. "I didn't get on with my sister either."

I gulped the last of my biscuit. "I have to be home for dinner."

"Just before you go." Margaret shuffled through some papers and wrote something on one of them. "I've been meaning to call in on your mother. You've saved me a trip." She handed me the paper. "Give this to your mother. I like to get to know the new neighbours. That's my home phone number and my mobile number."

"You have a cell phone?" I couldn't believe someone so old would be able to work one. I couldn't even work Katy's.

"Oh yes." She pointed to the smart phone sitting on the table. It was a fancy one just like Katy's. "New-fangled thing. I don't know how to use half the functions on it."

I smiled and put the paper in the pocket of my jeans.

Margaret walked me to the door. "It was nice to meet you, Laura."

"Thank you for the biscuit."

I started running again, as soon as I was outside. Margaret's house had a thick smell of perfume and I was glad to be out of it.

CHAPTER FOURTEEN

After dinner, Mum and Dad watched the news. Katy and I sat with them. She was curled up in a chair, reading a book, and I wasn't really paying much attention to the TV either. The newsreader's voice droned on in the background. That was until I heard his name.

"Missing boy Jacob Parata was last seen three days ago."

A picture of Jacob flashed up on the screen. I gasped and covered my mouth with my hand.

"What's wrong?" asked Mum. "You don't know that boy, do you?"

"No." I faked a cough.

"Police have identified Jacob as a person of

interest in their enquiry into the vandalism at Greenvale High School. Members of the public are asked to ring the number on screen if they have any information relating to his whereabouts."

Greenvale High School – that was Katy's new school! I leaned forward and stared at the TV. Mum gave me a funny look. I sat back with a thump and tried to look natural. Mum kept staring at me, so I picked at the edge of the Band-Aid on my finger, until she looked away.

A man and a woman appeared on the screen. The man looked just like Jacob and the woman had the same dark eyes. They had to be Jacob's parents.

"Jacob, we don't care what you've done. We just want you to come home." Jacob's mother had tears in her eyes.

"Please, if anyone watching knows anything, we're desperate," Jacob's dad said. "We're so worried."

I didn't know what to do. I needed time to think.

"Do you guys want some tea?" I asked.

Mum nodded.

"Coffee for me," said Dad.

Katy didn't look up from her book. "I want hot chocolate. Two sugars and make sure you heap the spoons. And see if there are any marshmallows, will you?"

I rolled my eyes, but nodded.

I flicked on the jug and started searching in the cupboard. What should I do? Should I tell on Jacob? I felt bad for his parents, they looked so upset. Jacob had seemed so angry when he thought I might tell on him, but maybe he was just scared? He'd been fine up until I suggested telling Katy about him.

"You need some help, Laura?" Dad called from the living room.

"No thanks." I poured out the drinks. My hands shook so much the cups rattled.

"Are you all right?" Mum asked as I slopped tea on the carpet.

"Yeah, what's the matter? Can't you even carry cups properly now?" Katy said.

"I'm fine."

"Why are you being so helpful, anyway? Are you hiding something?" Katy stared at me.

I glared at her and didn't answer.

"Laura, are you sure you don't know that boy?" Mum asked.

"No, Mum." I shook my head and looked away.

CHAPTER FIFTEEN

In the morning, I decided I had to find out more about what was going on with Jacob. I told Mum I was going for a walk.

"Don't go too far," Mum called after me. "You might get lost."

I sighed. "If I had a phone, you wouldn't have to worry."

"You know the rules. Not until you're thirteen."

I crept along the footpath until I was in front of the abandoned house, then slid in behind the trees. Once I was sure I couldn't be seen, I crouched down and shuffled along until I had a clear view of the house. Maybe Jacob would come outside. You could tell a lot about a person from how they acted when they didn't know they were being watched. Trespassers Club had taught me that.

I sat there for about fifteen minutes, but nothing happened so I stood up to leave. As I did, I smelt cigarette smoke and heard voices. I ducked back down behind the trees just in time. Two boys walked up towards the house. One of them was tall with big shoulders and a funny shaped nose. The other was shorter and fatter. He had flabby hands, his fingers splaying out like packets of sausages and his cheeks were a dark red, as if he had a permanent sunburn. Both of them were bigger than Jacob.

The taller one was lugging a backpack. They laughed and pushed each other, then one of them flicked his cigarette butt into the bushes near me.

"Parata better be here," the flat-nosed guy said.

"He will be; he's not stupid."

I strained to hear what they were saying as they moved further away. Jacob appeared in the doorway and the older boys moved in close, leaning over him. Jacob tried to back away, but they grabbed him, pushing him inside and slamming the door.

I crept up to the house. The windows were too high for me to see through. I jumped up, trying to get a glimpse, but I skidded on some damp moss and landed on my knees with a thud.

I looked around for something to stand on. There was a half-rotten wooden box in the bushes. I dragged it over and climbed up onto it.

The older boys pushed Jacob around. It looked like play fighting but just a little too rough, then the shorter boy opened the backpack. It was filled with cans of spray paint. He took one out and drew a big tag on the back wall. Jacob looked away and the other boys laughed.

I ducked down, as they turned to leave. They opened the door and I scrambled off the box, and around the corner of the house.

"Parata better make up his mind soon," one of them said.

"He will or he'll be sorry."

They both laughed as they walked away.

I shivered. I wasn't sure what was going on, but I could tell it wasn't good.

CHAPTER SIXTEEN

The next day, Mum started back at work, after taking time off for the move. Katy was going out too – into town with Amy, Hannah and some kids from their new school. I begged her to let me go with them, but she wouldn't even listen.

I wandered through the house, looking for something to do. Dad was working from home so that I wouldn't be alone – not that it made much difference. He was glued to his computer all morning.

I was heading into the kitchen to make a snack when I caught a glimpse of something moving outside the window. My stomach lurched. There was someone in the garden!

I looked closer. It was Jacob. I watched as he pulled an apple off one of the trees then he turned towards the window and saw me. I hesitated then waved at him. He frowned and waved back.

I unlocked the back door then beckoned to him, putting my finger to my lips. "You have to be quiet. My dad's inside."

"Okay." He came and stood just outside the door.

"Are you hungry?" I gestured towards the apple.

He shrugged. "I guess."

"You must be, living in that house all by yourself."

Jacob looked away and didn't answer.

"If you want, I could bring you some food."

He shook his head, as if he was going to refuse, then he stopped and sighed. "Yeah, that would be good, actually."

I wondered how long it had been since he'd had a proper meal. His face was pale, and he looked exhausted.

I took a breath. "I saw you on the news. Your parents–"

Jacob's eyes went wide. He dropped the apple and ran.

"Jacob, wait!" I called, but he disappeared over the fence at the edge of our garden. I sighed. How was I supposed to help him, if he wouldn't even talk to me?

"Who was that?" Dad came into the kitchen.

I spun round. "No-one."

"Then who were you talking to?"

"I wasn't. I was just singing."

Dad frowned. "Are you sure?"

"Yeah." I started humming to prove it.

Dad smiled and ruffled my hair. I turned and stared at the apple Jacob had dropped on the ground outside.

CHAPTER SEVENTEEN

"What are you doing, Laura?" Mum came into the kitchen the next day as I was packing up some food for Jacob.

I dropped the pear I was holding into my bag and closed the zip. "Just making a snack," I said.

"Why the bag?" Mum squinted at me.

"I thought I might eat outside," I mumbled.

"Mum!" Katy called from the other room.

Mum sighed. "What?" She turned to go and talk to Katy. I dodged out the back door while she was distracted.

I went over to the abandoned house and dumped the bag on the doorstep, then I walked away, making as much noise as possible so he'd know I was leaving. As soon as I was sure Jacob couldn't see me, I crept back behind the trees.

He opened the door and reached for the food.

"Why are you letting them get away with it!" I shouted.

Jacob darted backwards, like I'd thrown something at him. "W-what?"

"Those boys vandalized the school, didn't they? Now you're just letting them get away with it!"

Jacob's face flushed. "You don't understand! I don't have a choice."

"Of course you have a choice! What are you talking about?"

Jacob sighed, and stared at the ground for a moment. Finally, he shrugged. "It's a long story," he said. "You might as well come in." He stood back to let me into the house.

We sat down on the floor. I waited for Jacob to start talking, but instead he dived into the bag of food and stuffed a sandwich into his mouth.

"Sorry," he said, his mouth full. "I'm just really hungry."

It was gross to watch him eat. He was still chewing, and bits of lettuce fell from his lips, but he stuffed another bite into his mouth anyway. The mess made me glad I didn't have brothers.

"The police think you did the vandalism. But you didn't, did you?"

Jacob shook his head.

"It was those boys; the ones who were here the other day."

Jacob swallowed his mouthful but didn't answer.

"Then why don't you go to the police? If you told them–"

"I can't do that, Laura! They'd know I'd told. It would just make things worse."

"Are they bullying you?"

"They are my friends."

I frowned. "They didn't act like your friends. It looks like they just push you around."

"Yeah, well, no one else at school would even talk to me."

I knew how that felt. Katy was horrible to me, but she was the only friend I had.

There was a silence, and then Jacob sighed again. "They blamed me. They said they'd beat me up if I didn't go along with it. They even threatened my little sister."

"That's terrible!"

"Yeah, well, what can I do?"

"There must be some way of letting the police know who did it without actually telling them."

Jacob frowned, but I could see he was tempted by the idea. What we needed was a plan.

CHAPTER EIGHTEEN

"Will you come and see me tomorrow?" Jacob asked.

"Yeah, and I'll bring you more food." I started to leave, but Jacob called me back.

"Laura? You won't tell anyone, will you?"

I shook my head. "I promise."

As soon as I got home, I could see that Mum was in a mood. She was yelling at Katy. "For goodness sake, Katy, brush your hair before you come to dinner."

Katy scowled but went off to the bathroom anyway.

"And you Missy." Mum looked at me. "Don't think I don't know what you're up to."

I swallowed and blushed.

Mum set her mouth. "You said you were making a snack. I know we had more than two pears left, and you must have taken half a loaf of bread! What on earth did you do with it all?"

"I was hungry," I said.

"Really?" Mum looked like she didn't believe me. "So I suppose you don't want any dinner?"

"Yeah I do." My stomach grumbled as if it were listening.

Mum made a face, wrinkling up her nose. "You must be growing. Katy ate bread by the loaf when she was your age."

I nodded. "Must be." I would have to be more careful about what food I took. At least I'd got away with it for now.

I went to bed early that night and thought about Jacob's problem. Should I go to the police? That would be the easiest way to help him, but Jacob was scared of doing that. There had to be another way. It would be so much easier if Katy was here to think too, but Jacob had made me promise not to tell her.

"Hey, Munchkin." Katy appeared in the doorway.

"Don't call me Munchkin." I threw my pillow at her.

"Don't throw pillows! I'll tell on you."

"But you called me Munchkin."

"So? You are a Munchkin."

"I am not!" I glared at Katy.

She sat down on the end of my bed. "I know you've been going to that house. What do you do there anyway?"

I shrugged.

"You know, I should tell Mum and Dad." Katy fixed me with a stare.

I groaned. "No! Katy, please don't!"

"Why shouldn't I tell them?"

"Katy, don't! Please, I'll do anything." Saying this was always a mistake, but what else could I do?

Katy smiled and made a show of inspecting her nails. "Well … maybe I'll forget about it if you do my chores for a week?"

I sighed and nodded. I really was going to have to be much more careful.

CHAPTER NINETEEN

The doorbell rang. I ran to answer it, but I felt sick as I looked through the peephole. Jacob's parents were outside.

I backed away from the door. Did they know I was hiding Jacob? What should I do? I couldn't talk to them, I just couldn't.

The doorbell rang again, so I rushed into the bathroom and pulled the door across. I peered out through the tiny gap, waiting.

"Do I have to do everything in this house?" Katy stomped her way into the hall. "Hello?" she said as she opened the front door.

I held my breath.

"Are your parents home?" Jacob's mother asked.

Katy frowned. "Hey, you're the people who were on the news, aren't you?"

Jacob's mother nodded.

"My dad's home, but he's working," Katy said.

"Could you get him please?"

"Dad? Dad, can you come here?"

Dad came out into the hall. My mouth felt dry. What if Dad figured out where I'd been going in the afternoons?

"Hi." Dad seemed unsure of what to say.

"Dad, these are the people who were on the news. Remember?"

"Oh yes." Dad shook Jacob's father's hand. "Adam Benning."

"Brian Parata. This is my wife, Sandra."

"How can I help?"

Jacob's mother handed Dad a photo. "This is our son. Have you seen him?"

Dad shook his head. "I'm sorry, no."

"What about you?" Jacob's mother pushed the photo at Katy.

"I haven't seen him," Katy said.

"Take a good look. His name's Jacob. He's fourteen. He's a good boy. He's never done anything like this before. He's …" Her voice cracked. Jacob's dad put an arm around her.

"I'm sorry," Katy said. I could tell from her voice she was upset.

I closed my eyes and leant my head against the door. My skin felt all tingly and clammy, and my head hurt. Jacob's parents looked desperate. I felt awful for not telling them where he was.

"We just moved here. We haven't really been out much." Dad said. "You'd do better asking the neighbours."

"We will be. We're asking everyone in the area," Jacob's dad said.

Katy gave him back the photo, and he handed her a business card.

"If you do see or hear anything … please call us." He led Jacob's mother away, and Dad shut the door.

"Are you okay, love?" Dad asked Katy.

"Yeah, I'm fine." Katy shrugged. "They just looked so sad."

Dad gave a short laugh. "Just remember that if you ever feel like running away from home."

Katy rolled her eyes and let Dad put his arm around her. I watched them walking away. Finally, the hall was empty. I slipped out and went into my room. But Katy was waiting for me.

"What are you doing in here? Get out!" I said.

"Where were you just before?"

"Get out of my room!" I screamed.

"Not until you tell me where you were." Katy grabbed hold of my arm.

I tried to shake her off, but she held tight. "I was in the bathroom. What does it matter?"

"You're hiding something, aren't you?"

"No!" I twisted away from Katy's grip. "Leave me alone!"

"It has something to do with that boy, doesn't it?

"You know I'll find out even if you don't tell me," she said.

"Go away." I glared at her.

"Fine. I'm older and smarter than you. I'll figure it out myself." Katy stalked out of the room.

I shivered. Katy was right. Not about the being smarter than me part, but she almost always figured out what I was up to. I just had to hope Jacob and I could come up with a plan before she worked out what was going on.

CHAPTER TWENTY

Jacob opened the bag of food. The cat had come back and was curled up asleep in his lap. Its purring was so loud, it seemed to echo around the room.

Jacob gave me a puzzled frown as he pulled packets of jelly crystals and dried fruit out of the bag.

"I had to choose stuff that Mum wouldn't miss. She hasn't made jelly since she started working, and none of us like dried fruit all that much."

"Did you get in trouble?"

I shook my head. "No, not really, but I have to be more careful. Katy's already suspicious."

"Why? What happened?"

"She doesn't know anything for sure … but she's guessed something's going on. I had to climb out my window, so she wouldn't follow me."

"Clever." Jacob gave me a smile, and I felt myself blush.

I took a breath. "Listen, Jacob, your parents came to my house."

"What? Why?"

"They went to all the houses in the street. They're really upset."

Jacob groaned. "I didn't mean to hurt them, I was just scared."

He reached out and stroked the cat, but it was almost like he didn't even realise he was doing it. I watched as the cat stretched in its sleep and snuggled its head against his arm.

"I think you should go home, or phone them or something," I said.

"I can't! You know I can't." Jacob turned away from me.

"I'm sorry. It's just, you didn't see them! I had to hide because I was so scared I'd tell them."

"Don't, Laura. You promised!"

I shook my head. "I know. I didn't say anything and I won't, but …" I trailed off, unsure what else I could say to convince him.

"I will go home," he said. "I just have to figure out what to do first."

I sighed. "Look, I can't stay. I just came to drop off the food. Katy's making me do all her chores plus mine."

Jacob smiled and seemed to relax. "My brothers were like that. Don't worry; she'll grow out of it."

"Well I hope it's soon."

"Micky was twenty-two when he stopped, and Alan kept it up till he moved to London." Jacob laughed as I groaned. He picked up the cat and walked with me to the door. "Don't worry about bringing more food," he said. "I don't want you to get into trouble."

I smiled. "I'll bring stuff if I can. You'll starve otherwise."

I felt goosebumps rising on the back of my neck again as I walked home. It was like having a group of daddy long-legs crawling over my skin. I looked around. Was someone following me? Surely it wasn't Jacob this time. I couldn't see anyone, but they could be hiding. I broke into a run.

My feet slapped against the pavement, but I heard footsteps behind me. I spun around and saw a flash of blonde hair disappear behind a tree. Katy! Oh no! Had she seen me with Jacob? I slowed my pace. Maybe she was trying to find out what I was doing so she could get me in trouble with Mum and Dad. Well, I hadn't spent years playing Trespassers Club for nothing.

I changed direction and walked up towards the empty section next to our house. Katy followed me. I scaled the fence and dropped down on the other side. Before Katy had a chance to spot me, I crawled forward and crouched so I was hidden by the grass.

A second later I saw Katy struggling to squeeze around the end of the fence. I waited until she was standing upright again, looking for me.

"Why are you following me?" I jumped up out of the grass.

"What? I wasn't." Katy backed away but she was trapped by the fence.

"You were! I saw you."

Katy smiled. "It's a new game. It's called *Trespass on Laura*."

"Grow up, Katy." I turned away.

"Who was that boy you were with?"

I stopped and looked back at Katy.

She sneered at me. "What are you two doing, Laura? Playing house?"

"It's none of your business!" I gave Katy a dirty look and stormed off towards home.

"He's that boy from the TV, isn't he?"

I froze. Katy knew. No amount of doing her chores was going to fix this.

CHAPTER TWENTY-ONE

I turned to look at her. "No he's not," I said. I could feel a flush creeping up my neck.

Katy's eyes went wide. "You're lying."

"I'm not."

"You are! He really is that boy from the news, isn't he?"

I shook my head.

"Oh Laura, what have you done?"

"Nothing!"

"Yes, you have. You're hiding him, aren't you?"

"No, you're wrong." I felt sick and sweat dripped down my neck.

"If I'm wrong, you won't mind me going to that house." Katy turned to walk away.

"No, don't!" I grabbed Katy's arm and tried to pull her back.

"Why? If you're not hiding anything, why can't I go to the house?"

I stared at the ground. Tears stung the back of my eyes, but I didn't want to cry in front of Katy.

Her face softened. She sat down in the grass and patted the spot next to her. "Why don't you tell me what's going on?"

I reluctantly sat down with her. "I didn't mean to," I said. "It just happened."

"What happened?"

"I met Jacob at the house. I didn't know he'd run away until I saw him on the news." I wiped the back of my hand across my face, getting rid of the last trace that I'd been about to cry.

"Why didn't you tell me?"

"He was in trouble. I thought I could help."

Katy shook her head. "But Laura, you can't make friends with someone like that. He's wanted by the police!"

"It wasn't his fault!"

"Didn't you see how upset his parents were? You have to tell Mum and Dad."

"I can't! They'll go to the police and then Jacob will be arrested."

"So? That's what he deserves for vandalising the school." Katy stood up, stalking off towards home.

I jumped up and followed after her. "But it wasn't him! It was these two boys. One of them was short and he had these really red cheeks and the other was tall and had a funny nose, and–"

"Wait ..." Katy stopped and turned to stare at me. "What were these boys' names?"

I shook my head. "I don't know. Jacob never told me."

Katy frowned. "It's just ... when I went into town with Amy and Hannah the other day, we met some boys from Greenvale High. They looked just like that." Katy bit her lip. "But they were really mean and–"

"That will be them! They're bullying Jacob. They're trying to make him take the blame for the vandalism."

Katy was quiet for a moment. "You know what? Now that I think about it, they had paint on their hands."

"Then it was definitely them!"

Katy shook her head. "That's what they call circumstantial evidence, Laura. It doesn't prove anything." She paused, thinking. "But it is enough to make me think *maybe* Jacob is innocent."

I bounced on the balls of my feet. "So, you won't tell Mum and Dad?"

Katy gave a half-smile. "I don't know. I think I need to talk to Jacob."

CHAPTER TWENTY-TWO

I pushed the door open. I couldn't see Jacob at first, and I wondered if he'd taken off. "Jacob?" I called.

Katy shivered. "This place gives me the creeps."

Jacob came out of the bedroom. "I thought you had to do your sister's chores …" He stopped as he saw Katy. "What'd you bring her for? You promised you wouldn't tell anyone!"

"I didn't, but–"

"I never should have trusted you." He grabbed his jacket, ready to leave.

Katy blocked his way. "Laura didn't tell me anything. I saw you at the door when she left."

"Yeah right." Jacob stepped forward, like he was going to push past Katy, but she stood her ground, lifting her chin and crossing her arms. They stared at each other for a moment.

Jacob was the first to look away. "Are you going to tell?"

Katy shrugged. "I haven't decided yet."

"I didn't do it," Jacob mumbled.

"Well if it wasn't you, who was it?" Katy raised her eyebrows.

Jacob shrugged. He pulled at his fringe, avoiding looking at Katy.

"As far as I can gather," Katy said, "it was Mark Cutter and David Hodgson."

Jacob gaped at her. "How did you know?"

"So it was them?"

Jacob hesitated, then he nodded. He let out a breath and seemed to deflate, as if he could finally relax a little now everything was out in the open.

"If you didn't do it, why did you run away?" Katy asked.

Jacob kicked the floor and didn't answer.

Katy sighed. "Okay, we'll do this the hard way. Laura said they're trying to make you take the blame. Is that why you ran away?"

Jacob nodded.

"But why you?" Katy asked.

"I was there … but I didn't do any of it, I swear." Jacob's words came out in a rush, tripping over each other.

"A likely story," Katy said, sarcastically. She narrowed her eyes. "Why do they need someone to take the fall? Why can't they just say nothing?"

Jacob stared at his feet. "The police found Mark's hoodie. He must have dropped it. His Mum had sewn his name into it." Jacob smiled slightly. "Anyway, when they talked to him, Mark told them he'd lent it to me and David backed him up. He rang me after the police left and told me he'd smash me if I didn't take the blame." Jacob glanced at me, then looked back at Katy. "He said he'd kidnap my little sister, Michelle. She's only about Laura's age. I didn't think he'd really do it, but then she came home from school with bruises on her arms and a message from him." He swallowed. "That's when I ran away."

Katy glanced at me as well, and she looked nervous. "How'd Mark find you?" she asked.

"All the kids around here know this house. I should have hidden somewhere better."

"I see."

Jacob shifted his feet, still not looking at Katy. "So, are you going to tell?"

"I don't know." Katy sat down. "I think you better tell me the whole story."

CHAPTER TWENTY-THREE

Katy asked lots of questions. Jacob seemed reluctant to answer some of them at first, but the more he talked the easier it seemed to get.

"When are Mark and David coming back?" Katy asked.

"They said a couple of days, so maybe tomorrow?"

Katy nodded. "I think I should be here when they come."

"Me too," I said.

"No, Laura." Katy rolled her eyes. "It's too dangerous."

"But–" I started.

"I don't think either of you should come."

Katy stared at Jacob and raised her eyebrows again. "I think it would be safer if I'm here. I'll stay outside, but I can call for help if you need it."

Jacob hesitated, then shrugged, defeated. "Fine. But stay out of sight."

Katy got up to leave, and Jacob walked over to the door with us.

"Hey, Katy? Thanks."

She smiled, and we started off towards home.

I snuck looks at Katy a couple of times on the way back, but she didn't notice. She looked as if she was too busy thinking. I felt side-lined. I was glad Katy was helping Jacob, but I didn't like the way she'd just taken over. I thought I'd been doing a good job of looking after Jacob by myself.

"You know, you really should have told me earlier," she said suddenly.

"Huh?"

"You should have told me!" she snapped. "This isn't one of your games, Laura. Jacob needs help."

"I was trying to help him."

"You're ten. You can't handle something like this by yourself."

I scowled at Katy. "Jacob asked me not to tell anyone."

"I'm not just *anyone*; I'm your sister! You should have told me."

"But …" I couldn't think of anything else to say. Maybe Katy was right, but I'd been doing what Jacob wanted.

Katy took off towards the house, her ponytail swinging behind her. "Hurry up. Mum will be wondering where we are."

I sighed and followed after her.

CHAPTER TWENTY-FOUR

I waited until Katy left the house the next day, then snuck out my window. I caught up with her pretty quickly, but I hung back, stalking her. She was my target and I was a spy sent to track her.

She settled down by the side of the abandoned house and I crept in behind her. She spun around, her eyes wide. "I told you not to come, Laura!" she hissed.

I sat down next to her. "You might need help."

"No! I want you to go home now."

"Shhh!" I could smell cigarette smoke – Mark and David must be in the garden.

Katy and I shrank back against the side of the house, as they made their way through the mud.

They didn't seem to have as much trouble with it as I had, walking easily through the slushy bits.

Jacob came outside when they reached the door, and one of the boys clapped him on the shoulder.

"Parata, good to see you," he said. His voice had a false cheery sound to it which made my stomach feel wobbly.

"That's David," Katy whispered. "The shorter one's Mark."

I nodded then put a finger to my lips.

"So? What are you gonna do?" Mark moved in close to Jacob, leaning over him.

Jacob fidgeted and looked around. "Come in," he said eventually. He glanced our way before going inside, but I don't think he could see us.

Katy and I ran to the window, clambering up on the rotten box.

"What are they saying?" Katy gripped my arm.

"I don't know." I pressed my ear to the edge of the window.

"It looks like he's stalling. I think he needs … Arghh!"

Katy screamed as the box gave way beneath us. I fell backwards, hitting my head. Katy tumbled down on top of me. I tried to sit up, but the ground felt like it was moving.

"Quickly, Laura!" Katy yanked me to my feet and dragged me behind the trees. A second later the boys appeared on the doorstep.

"What was that? Is someone out here?" Mark's voice was a low growl.

Jacob's face was pale as he scanned the garden. "No … I don't know." Jacob shifted his feet and looked away.

Mark seemed to look straight at us. I closed my eyes and held my breath, willing him not to see us. Finally, I heard footsteps moving away.

Katy touched my arm. "It's all right. They've gone back inside. Is your head okay?"

I opened my eyes and nodded.

Katy smiled. "Come on. I've got an idea."

CHAPTER TWENTY-FIVE

Katy made me wait while she ran up to the garage.

"Here we go," she said when she came back. She held out a skipping rope.

I frowned. "What are you going to do with that?" I asked.

"You'll see."

Katy stretched out the rope and started jumping. I rubbed my head where I'd bumped it and sat down on the footpath. I couldn't work out what Katy was doing. How could this possibly help Jacob?

I froze as Mark and David came out on to the street. Should I run? I looked at Katy, but she didn't seem at all worried.

She stopped jumping. "Mark? David? What are you doing here?"

"Katy?" Mark looked puzzled.

Katy nodded towards me. "My mum made me babysit my little sister. It's so boring."

The boys stared at me, which made me want to squirm.

"We just moved here," Katy said. "Do you guys live nearby?"

"We're just visiting a friend," David said.

Katy looked at me and jerked her head towards our house. When I didn't move, she did it again. It took me a moment to realise she was trying to get rid of me.

I stood up. "I'm going to the loo," I mumbled.

I walked half-way up our driveway then crouched down and peered back at the street. Katy giggled and tucked her hair behind her ear. Was she *flirting*? I couldn't believe it. What on earth did she think she was doing? I turned and ran up to the house.

Katy joined me a few minutes later. "They saw you watching," she said. "But it's okay. I told them you're just a kid and you like to spy on me."

I scowled at her, but she just laughed and patted me on the head. "I didn't mean it; I just had to tell them something."

"You were flirting with them!"

Katy shrugged. "Not really. I was just pretending to, so they'd ask me to go into town with them."

"That's awful!"

"But don't you see? If I can make friends with

them then maybe I can find some evidence against them!"

"I don't think–"

"Look, don't worry about it. I've got it sorted. Now I'm going back to check on Jacob. Do you want to come?"

I frowned but trailed after Katy again anyway.

CHAPTER TWENTY-SIX

"I don't like it." Jacob turned away from us.

Katy clicked her tongue, irritated. "It'll be fine. We'll be in town; there'll be heaps of people around."

"No. It's too dangerous. We'll have to think of something else."

Katy snorted "We've been trying to think of something else and no-one's come up with anything."

Jacob shook his head. "No, I'm not going to let you do it."

Katy raised her eyebrows. "*Let* me do it?"

Jacob stared at her for a moment, then shrugged and looked away.

Katy sighed. "Well, what if I asked my friends to come with me? I'd probably have to tell them a bit about what's going on though."

Jacob hesitated then nodded. "Okay, I guess that could work."

"Good."

I sat up. "I could come too. I could–"

"NO!" Jacob and Katy said together. They looked at each other and laughed. I slumped back down and scowled at them. They didn't notice.

Katy stood up. "Come on, Laura. We'd better get home."

I stood too and stropped out. I paused on the doorstep and looked back. Jacob glanced questioningly at Katy, and she shrugged. I bit my lip and turned away.

As soon as we got home, Katy rang Amy. I stood outside her bedroom door and listened.

"You remember those guys we met the other day …? Yeah, them." Katy paused and laughed at something Amy said. "Well, we've got to go into town with them tomorrow."

I peered around the door.

Katy scrunched up her face. "I know, I know, I didn't like them either." She sighed. "I can't tell you now, but I promise I'll explain tomorrow … Okay, meet you at the train station."

I didn't wait for her to ring Hannah. Instead, I went into my room, climbed onto the bed and stared at the wall. A few minutes later Katy came in.

"Hey Munchkin, are you okay?"

I kept staring at the wall.

She sat down on the end of my bed. "No pillow throwing? You must be upset."

I tried to suppress a smile.

"I know you feel like you're being left out, but I just want to protect you."

I nodded but didn't say anything. I could feel tears forming.

Katy reached into her pocket. "How about this: I'll leave you my cell phone and I'll message you from Hannah's phone to let you know what's happening?"

"Really?" I took the phone and held it carefully. "You have to tell me everything though!"

Katy smiled and ruffled my hair. "Remember to keep it out of sight. We don't want Mum and Dad getting suspicious."

I smiled and slipped the phone into my bedside cabinet drawer.

CHAPTER TWENTY-SEVEN

Mum shook me awake the next morning and pulled off the bedclothes. “Come on, Laura, time to get up. We’re going shoe shopping.”

“But–”

“No excuses. Come on.”

“But Katy–”

“Katy’s gone into town with Amy and Hannah.”

I sat up and rubbed my eyes. “But–”

“No ‘buts’. You need new school shoes. Five minutes and you better be in the kitchen eating breakfast.” Mum didn’t stop to wait for an answer.

I pulled Katy’s phone out of the bedside cabinet drawer and pressed buttons at random. How did I put it on silent? Nothing seemed to work. I put it back in the drawer. I hated having to leave it behind, but I couldn't see another option.

Mum and I took the bus into town. I peered out the window as we passed the railway station but I didn't spot Katy. I thought about all the messages she must be sending me and hoped she was okay.

The bus pulled in at our stop, and I glanced down the street. I sat up. Was that Amy? I could only see the girl from the back but the red plait snaking its way round the girl's neck looked like Amy's.

"Hurry up, Laura." Mum took hold of my arm, guiding me off the bus.

"Look, Mum. I think that's Katy." I pointed to the group of three girls.

"Well it's a good thing we're going the other way." Mum steered me away.

"But, Mum! Can't we just say hi?"

Mum stopped and looked at me. "Laura, when you're Katy's age you'll understand."

"But–"

Mum wasn't listening. She pulled me away from Katy, towards the shoe shop.

CHAPTER TWENTY-EIGHT

I dropped my new shoes in the hall, rushed into my bedroom and grabbed Katy's phone. Four new messages. What was her password again? I should have asked her to write it down. The phone beeped, and I nearly dropped it.

"Laura?" Mum stuck her head round the door.

I stuffed the phone under my pillow. "Yeah?"

"Did you hear that?"

I shrugged. "Hear what?"

"It sounded like Katy's phone. I hope she hasn't left it behind. Maybe I should ring her to check."

"No!"

Mum stared at me. "Why not?"

"Well, you said before that she didn't want to be bothered. If she's left it behind, she'll get it when she comes home."

Mum looked puzzled. "All right."

I waited till Mum was gone then pulled the phone out from under my pillow. A moment later it rang. Mum. Why couldn't she just listen to me, and leave Katy alone? I stuffed the phone back under my pillow and held my breath. Hopefully Mum couldn't tell the noise was coming from my room. I counted the rings. After six, it finally stopped.

I pulled it out and looked at it. Five new messages and one missed call. I keyed in the password and pulled up the message list. Four from Hannah, one missed call from home. And a video message from David Hodgson ...

What was he doing messaging Katy? I opened the message. It was blurry and jerking but I could just make it out. The phone weaved around to show David. His arm stretched out to hold the phone and film himself. He was wearing a hoodie that almost covered his face, but it was still obviously him. I peered at the background. It looked like he was in front of some school buildings.

The phone swung round again to show Jacob arguing with Mark. The sound was too distorted to understand, but Jacob kept shaking his head and trying to back away.

Mark grabbed him and shoved the spray can into his hand then pushed him towards one of the school walls. Jacob was shaking. Mark and David yelled at him but he just stood there. Finally Mark grabbed the can off him and drew a tag himself. I watched as Jacob ran away, then I closed the video. Jacob had to see this.

CHAPTER TWENTY-NINE

Jacob stared at the screen. "I didn't realise David had filmed us."

"But don't you see what this means?" I waved the phone in his face. "The video shows you didn't do it."

"Yeah?" Jacob shrugged.

"If we just take this to the police then–"

"No!"

"Why not? If we show them–"

"I told you before," Jacob said, "it would just make this worse if I went to the police. For Katy now too."

"But–"

"There you are." Katy walked in the door. "Why didn't you message back?"

"Look at this." I showed Katy the video.

"Why did he send this to me?" she said when she'd finished watching. "He barely even spoke to me all day. He must have sent it after we left."

"I think we should take it to the police," I said.

Katy nodded. "Yeah, we definitely should."

Jacob grabbed the phone off Katy. "No-one's going to the police. They'd know it was us."

"So? I'm not scared of them." Katy reached for her phone.

Jacob held it above his head. "Well you should be."

Katy frowned. "What are you so worried about? I went into town with them and I was fine."

"You were lucky."

"You sound like my Mum."

"Grow up, Katy, this isn't a game."

They glared at each other. I stepped backwards and tried to disappear into the wall. There was a horrible silence then Katy snatched her phone off Jacob and stormed out of the room.

Jacob slumped down on the couch and put his head in his hands.

I crept forward. "She doesn't stay mad for long."

"What?" Jacob looked up and I could tell he'd forgotten I was there.

"She doesn't stay mad for long. Give her a couple of hours and she'll calm down."

"Yeah, whatever." Jacob looked away.

"I'll see you later, then," I said. Jacob didn't look up as I left.

CHAPTER THIRTY

"Katy?" I knocked on her bedroom door, but she didn't answer. "Katy?" I called again. When I still got no response, I pushed the door open. She was lying on the bed facing the wall.

I sat down on the end of the bed. "Are you sulking?"

"No." Her voice had a crack in it.

"Come on, Katy. We have to help Jacob."

"That's what I was trying to do! Then he goes and yells at me."

"He's just scared. Mark and David will beat him up if they found out he told. Or worse, they might hurt his sister too."

"He still didn't have to yell at me."

I poked Katy's shoulder until she sat up. Her eyes were all red-rimmed and she wouldn't look at me.

I put my arm around her. "You yell at me all the time and I forgive you."

She laughed. "That's true, Munchkin."

"So you'll help Jacob?"

"Yeah, okay. I'll help him."

We watched the video again, but I didn't spot anything new. "We could send it to the principal?" I said. "Then she could give it to the police."

Katy rolled her eyes. "We don't have the principal's phone number."

We both jumped as her phone rang again.

"It could be them," I whispered.

Katy showed me the caller ID. It was Amy.

"Hello?" Katy made a face at me. "I know. He sent me it to me too." She sighed. "Yeah, but Jacob won't let us … No, Laura and I have just been talking about that." She paused, twisting the end of her hair around her finger as she listened. "Yeah, maybe you can talk some sense into him … Okay, see you then." Katy put the phone down. "Amy and Hannah are going to come over tomorrow. They might be able to talk Jacob round."

I scowled. "I don't think that'll work. Jacob will probably just get annoyed."

"Don't be so negative! Amy can be very persuasive."

"But–"

Katy wasn't listening. "I'm starved," she said. "Let's go see if dinner's ready."

I had a bad feeling about this.

CHAPTER THIRTY-ONE

"What are they doing here?" Jacob scowled at Amy and Hannah.

"Don't be so rude. They're here to help," Katy said.

"I don't want their help. I want you all to leave."

Katy glared at Jacob. Amy and Hannah looked at each other.

"We can go," Amy said. "We don't have to be here."

"Don't be silly." Katy tossed her hair back over her shoulders. "Amy and Hannah agree with me. We all think you should go to the police, right?" Katy glanced at the girls, but Amy shuffled her feet and looked away. Hannah stared at the ceiling.

Jacob looked really angry. "Shove off. It's none of your business."

"You've made it our business!"

"What happens to my sister if you go to the police? Who's going to look after her?"

Katy clicked her tongue. "It was probably just an empty threat. They wouldn't really do something like that."

"You don't know them like I do!" Jacob shouted.

I knew how he felt. If Katy felt like taking over she would and there was nothing he could do about it. I sighed for him, then glanced out the window, and my stomach did a flip-flop. Mark and David were walking up the garden!

"Guys, look!" I shrieked. There was a horrible silence then everyone was talking at once.

"-Climb out the window-"

"-Where's the back door-"

"-Behind the couch-"

"Stop!" Jacob hissed. "Hide in the other room."

He shoved the door to the bedroom open and we all clambered through. "Now keep quiet," he said as he pulled the door closed again.

I was shaking, and I felt cold. The other girls crammed against the door to listen, but I stood back. I just wanted to go home.

Mark and David were yelling at Jacob. "Stop mucking around. Are you going to take the blame or not?"

Jacob stuttered. It seemed like he couldn't get any words out.

"This is it, Parata. This is your last chance."

There was a big crash. I covered my face with my hands as I imagined them hitting Jacob. Katy put her arm around me and Amy and Hannah backed away from the door.

Everything went really quiet. The other girls inched forward, listening.

Suddenly, there was a clatter outside the window, and a shape hurtled off the sill onto the bunk-beds.

Squeeeak … Thump … Thump …

Oh no! The cat was back!

"What was that?" Mark yelled

I pulled the other girls away from the door and scanned the room for a place to hide.

"It's nothing, it's just a cat." Jacob said.

"Get in the wardrobe," I whispered to Katy.

We piled in and closed the door. It smelt of mould and mothballs and we were squished in amongst dusty jackets and coats.

I heard the bedroom door open. Hannah made a face like she was going to sneeze. I clapped a hand over her mouth and my finger hit her braces hard. I gritted my teeth, trying not to make a noise.

"He's right, it's just a cat," Mark said.

"Mark, can we go and see if Katy's home?" David asked. "Parata can wait."

"Yeah, all right. Come on."

A moment later Jacob pulled the wardrobe door open. He looked pale, and he held his arm like it was hurting. "They're gone," he said.

"I know." Katy pushed Jacob out of the way.

"They're going to our house. We'll have to hurry."

Katy and the other girls ran off.

I looked at Jacob. "Are you okay?"

"I'm fine," he said, but it obviously wasn't true. "Just go."

I stared at him, but he turned away.

CHAPTER THIRTY-TWO

I took off after the other girls. We raced through the neighbours' back gardens, not even trying to stay hidden. Katy ran ahead of us, and we got home just after the boys arrived.

"Hi." Katy was out of breath. "We've just been to the shop. You remember Amy and Hannah, don't you?"

"Yeah, hi." Mark glanced at Amy and Hannah, then looked at me. I squirmed.

"Laura," Katy said. "Why don't you go play in the garden?"

Normally I would have protested, but I wanted an excuse to get away from Mark and David. I went around the side of the house and crouched down out of sight. If I strained, I could just hear what they were saying.

"Hey, why'd you send us that video?" Katy asked.

"What video?" Mark sounded angry.

"David sent us all a video message," Amy said.

"What was in it?"

"It was–"

Katy cut across Hannah. "It was too blurry to tell really. I need a better phone."

"Yeah, me too," Amy and Hannah said together.

"So, do you want to come inside?" Katy asked.

"Nah, we've got stuff to do. See ya later," Mark said.

"Yeah, see ya."

I shrunk back against the house as Mark and David came down the path. Suddenly, Mark rounded on David and grabbed his arm. I jumped and covered my mouth with my hand.

"What did you think you were doing sending them that video?" Mark got right in David's face as he spoke.

David gaped at him, his mouth popping like a fish.

"Not only are you stupid enough to film us, but then you go and send it to them. Do you know how much trouble we could get in?" Mark pushed David up the path towards me.

I crawled backwards, trying to stay hidden.

"Well if you hadn't dropped your stupid hoodie–"

"That was an accident." Mark twisted David's arm. "Are you so thick you can't see what'll happen?

We'd be arrested! Why the hell did you do it?"

"I dunno." David tried to pull away, kicking up gravel off the path as he did.

A piece stung my arm, and I bit my lip trying to stay quiet.

"What? You thought they'd be impressed? You thought they might actually like you?" Mark sneered.

David shrugged. "Yeah, maybe."

"Idiot! You're as bad as Parata."

"I didn't mean to. I just thought …" David looked embarrassed. I made a face at his back. Katy deserved better.

"Yeah, I know what you thought. You're just lucky they couldn't see it properly." Mark let go of David and walked away. "Come on, let's get out of …" Mark stopped suddenly. I froze again as he turned back to face David.

"You didn't send it to anyone else, did you?" he asked.

David looked sick. He didn't answer.

"Are you really that stupid?" Mark shook his head. He turned away and David followed at his heels like a puppy.

I waited until they were gone then ran up to the house. I had to tell the others about this.

CHAPTER THIRTY-THREE

"Ew, David likes you, Katy," Hannah giggled.

"He sent it to you guys too." Katy had gone pink.

"Anyway," Amy rolled her eyes, "I think we should tell Jacob about this. If David's sent the video to other people, then we might be able to go to the police after all. David and Mark would have no way of knowing who took it."

"Jacob won't agree to that," Katy said. "He's being stubborn."

Amy clicked her tongue. "Well, we have to try."

They got up and headed out, but I hung back.

"Are you coming, Laura?" Amy asked.

I shook my head. Amy shrugged and followed after the others.

I went outside and watched as they went down to the street. Something Katy had said before had gotten to me. *"This isn't one of your games, Laura. Jacob needs help."* I hated the way the other girls had just taken over, but Katy was right, I had been treating it as a game. Of course I'd been trying to help Jacob as well, but it had just seemed like such a good adventure.

I decided I would leave Jacob's problem to the older girls. It was too much stress and maybe playing by myself wasn't so bad after all.

I set off through the neighbours' back gardens. In my head I was a tiger, searching for prey. I kept low to the ground, stalking, cat-like. I saw something moving ahead of me. I dropped down even lower and shuffled forward, ready to pounce, then leapt. My hands closed on a plastic bag. I laughed and let it go.

"Hello, Laura."

I looked up. There was the old lady again.

"Margaret?" I said.

"Yes, that's right, love. How's the finger doing?"

I held up my hand, remembering my ripped nails. "It's okay. All better now."

Margaret smiled. "Would you like to come inside?"

I remembered the thick smell of perfume and hesitated.

"I've got some more of those biscuits you liked," she added.

"Okay, then."

I followed her inside. It seemed like she'd got even more ornaments and plates since I was last there. I couldn't help staring.

"I know it's a bit cluttered," Margaret said when she saw me looking. "You get like that at my age."

I bit back an urge to ask her how old she was. "I like it," I said. "Mum doesn't like ornaments. She likes *nice clean surfaces.*"

Margaret laughed at my imitation of Mum's voice. "How is your mother?" she asked.

"She's all right. Quite busy with work."

"You know, she never phoned me."

I frowned. Why would Mum be phoning Margaret? I clapped my hands over my mouth. I'd forgotten to give Mum Margaret's number.

Margaret laughed. "It's all right, Laura. I can't tell you how many times I sent notes home with pupils and they never got to the parents …"

I stood up. Of course! Why hadn't I thought of it before? "I'm sorry, I have to go," I said and rushed out.

CHAPTER THIRTY-FOUR

I ran out into Margaret's front garden and stopped with a jolt. Mark and David were standing in front of the house. I watched as Mark drew a big tag on the wall.

"That'll teach her to give me detention," Mark said. He laughed as David took the spray can.

I stepped backwards and something cracked under my foot. Mark looked straight at me. I shrieked and ran.

"Grab her! Don't let her get away!" Mark yelled.

I tripped and fell forwards. A hand closed round my arm.

"Help! Help!" I screamed.

"Shut up, will ya?" David pulled me to my feet and put a hand over my mouth.

I twisted and squirmed, but David gripped me tighter, so I kicked and hit out at him.

"Stop it!" Mark grabbed my arms and held tight. They both dodged out of the way of my kicks.

"The kitten bites." Mark laughed at me.

That seemed like a good idea. I bit down hard on David's hand. He yelped and let go. I tried to run but Mark held strong. "You're not going anywhere."

"Let me go! I'll tell Katy," I said.

"No, you won't. You're Katy's sister, right?"

"Yeah." I stopped wriggling. My arms were starting to hurt.

"What's your name?" Mark asked.

"Laura."

"Okay, Laura. You see, the old lady who lives at this house asked us to draw these pictures on her house. She wanted it to look more interesting. Isn't that right, David?"

"Yeah … Yeah, that's right." David rubbed his hand where I'd bit him.

"I don't believe you. Let me go!" I screamed.

Mark narrowed his eyes. "Okay then, David and I know where you live. If you tell anyone we'll come and break every window in your house and you don't even want to know what we'll do to Katy."

"Don't! My parents would be so mad!"

"So don't tell anyone."

I glared at him but nodded reluctantly.

"Okay, then." Mark let go of my arms. "You can go."

I took off running and didn't stop till I got home.

CHAPTER THIRTY-FIVE

I slammed my bedroom door behind me, and leaned against it, trying to catch my breath. Finally, my breathing slowed, but my hands wouldn't stop shaking. I rubbed at my arms. They were coming up all red. I had to stop Mark, I just had to! I couldn't believe he'd done that to Margaret. What would I do if she asked me about it?

I searched through the pile of clothes on the chair in my room. Where were my jeans? They had to be there. My stomach seemed to drop down through my body to my feet. Oh no! I'd put them in the wash. I crossed my fingers and looked in my dirty clothes basket. It was empty.

I pulled my sleeves down as far as they would go

and ran out into the kitchen. "Mum! Mum!"

"Shhh, Laura. Use your inside voice." Mum was in the laundry.

"You haven't done the washing yet, have you?"

"Yes, I have actually."

"Oh no!" I put my head in my hands.

"How many times have I told you to empty your pockets before you put things in the wash?"

"Too many," I chimed in Mum's voice.

"Hmm. Well you're lucky I checked before I started the load. Here you go." Mum handed me the collection of things from my pockets.

I sorted through the coins and pieces of paper. There was Margaret's number!

"Thank you, Mum." I gave her a kiss on the cheek and ran out.

CHAPTER THIRTY-SIX

"Katy …? Katy, look what I've got!"

"She's not here," Jacob said as I came through the door. "They went to the shops. They kept harping on about going to the police. They don't have any other ideas."

"Look at this." I held out the phone number.

"What happened to your arms? They're all blue!"

I stretched out my arm to look. Purpley-blue bits were coming up amongst the red. I looked like an overripe peach. "Oh, that. Mark did it."

"What?!"

"I caught him and David tagging."

"What? Where?"

"At Margaret's house. Mark said he'd break all the windows at my house if I told. And they threatened Katy."

"Did they hurt you?"

"Nah, I'm okay." I rubbed my arms. They were sore, but they didn't feel too bad now.

"Were you scared?"

"No," I lied.

Jacob smiled. "I'm scared of them."

"Yeah, okay, maybe I was scared, but I bit David."

"What? You bit him?" Jacob laughed.

I joined in, laughing too. "Anyway, look at this." I held out the phone number again.

"What is it?"

"Margaret's a teacher at your school. We can send her the video and she can take it to the police."

"I don't know …"

"Come on! David sent out more than one copy. He'll never know who it was."

"Yeah, I s'pose," Jacob said after a pause, "but Katy's number will come up on Margaret's phone."

"No, it won't. Mum made Katy list her number as private so if she rang someone by mistake they wouldn't get her number."

"But what if Margaret doesn't have a video phone? What do we do then?"

"I saw her phone. It was the same one as Katy's."

Jacob started to smile. "You've done it, Laura. I can go home. It's all over!"

"Not yet, it isn't. We still have to send the message."

"Yeah, but it will be over soon. Come on, let's go find Katy."

CHAPTER THIRTY-SEVEN

"There she is." I pointed over to the shops.

Jacob ran across the road ahead of me. "We need your phone, Katy," he called.

"Why?" she asked.

"We'll explain later." Jacob took the phone out of her hand. "Here you go, Laura."

"Hey! Give that back." Katy tried to grab the phone, but Jacob pushed her away.

"Go on, send it, Laura."

I fumbled with the phone, unsure how to forward a message on it.

Jacob laughed. "Okay, I'll do it." He keyed in the number and pressed send. My breath came out in a rush. Jacob smiled at me.

"Will someone please tell me what's going on?" Katy folded her arms.

"Yeah!" added Amy and Hannah together.

Jacob and I both laughed.

I explained about Margaret's phone number, then about me finding Mark and David tagging, as we walked back towards the house.

Katy gave me a hug. "You were so brave!"

I shrugged. "I don't think they would have let me go if I wasn't your sister."

"So, you can go home now, Jacob," Amy said.

"Not just yet." Jacob pulled his hoodie further down over his face. "Can you guys watch the news for the next couple of days? Let me know if there's anything about the vandalism. I don't want to go home until I know Margaret's gone to the police."

"Okay, we'll watch tonight," I said.

Katy stopped outside home. "You guys go on up. I'm just going to walk Jacob back to the house," she said.

Amy and Hannah exchanged a look as Jacob and Katy walked away. I watched until they went out of view, then ran up the path to our house.

CHAPTER THIRTY-EIGHT

"What are you two up to?" Mum asked.

"Just waiting for the news to come on." Katy plonked herself down on the couch. I sat next to her.

"You've never been interested in the news before. What are you hiding?"

"Nothing, Mum."

Mum sighed. "All right …"

"Shhh! It's on." I pointed to the TV.

Katy and I leant forward every time a new story started, then sat back when it wasn't about Jacob. Mum kept giving us funny looks, but we just smiled at her each time she did.

The picture on screen went back to the female newsreader. "There's been a new development in the case of the vandalism at Greenvale High School …"

I gasped.

"Shhh, Laura!" Katy jabbed me in the ribs.

"What's going on? Do you two know something about this?" Mum asked.

"No, I just want to hear what they're saying." Katy gave me a look.

The video from Katy's phone flashed up on the screen. The faces were blanked out but it was still recognizable. Katy squeezed my hand.

"…two fifteen-year-olds were arrested after this video came to the attention of the police. The video was handed in to police by someone wishing to remain anonymous …"

Katy jumped up. "This is boring. Come on, Laura."

"But–" I started.

"I said, come on Laura!"

I followed Katy into my bedroom.

"I going to go tell Jacob," she whispered. "You make sure Mum and Dad don't know I'm gone."

"What? Now? Why don't you wait and we can go in the morning."

"No, Jacob will want to know now. If Mum and Dad ask, say I had a headache and went to bed."

I shook my head. "No. I'm coming with you."

Katy opened her mouth like she was going to argue then she sighed. "Okay. Come on, I'll help you down." She swung her legs out over the windowsill and jumped out, then reached up to help me.

CHAPTER THIRTY-NINE

Katy held my hand as we walked up through the abandoned house's garden, so I wouldn't slip, but I could feel her shivering.

"Are you cold?" I whispered.

"What?" She glanced over at me. "Nah, it's just kind of creepy in the dark."

I laughed. "Katy, it's six-thirty. It's still light out."

Katy shrugged. "You know what I mean."

I knocked on the door of the house. "Jacob?" I called. "Jacob? It's just us."

There was a shuffling noise inside, then Jacob came to the door, wrapped in a bright green sleeping bag. He looked like a giant caterpillar winding itself into a cocoon.

He rubbed at his eyes. "What's wrong? Mark didn't come back, did he?"

I shook my head. "No, it's good news."

"What? What's happened?"

Katy rolled her eyes. "Let us in and we'll tell you."

Jacob stood back and we went inside. It was cold in the house at night. Outside it hadn't been too bad but the walls seemed to trap in all the cold air. I almost made the mistake of trying to turn on the heater, then remembered there was no power.

Katy and I sat down on the couch.

"So?" Jacob crossed his arms under the sleeping bag.

"You tell him, Laura." Katy smiled at me.

I took a breath. "We saw it on the news. Mark and David have been arrested. They played the video and everything!"

Jacob went really still. For a second, I thought he hadn't heard me then he started laughing. He dragged his hands down over his face.

"This is awesome. I can go home!" He threw the sleeping bag off and kicked it. "No more hiding out in this dump. No more eating jelly crystals and–"

Katy cleared her throat.

Jacob looked up at her. "What?"

"You could at least say thank you." Katy's voice was cross, but she couldn't help smiling.

Jacob laughed. "Thank you, thank you, thank you." He picked me up and spun me round on the spot.

"Put me down!" I screamed.

He dropped me back down on the couch and moved towards Katy.

"Pick me up and I'll do worse than scream," she said.

Jacob gave her a hug instead. When he let go, they both blushed and wouldn't look at each other.

Katy shifted her feet then glanced at me. "Come on," she said. "We'd better get home before Mum and Dad notice we're gone."

"True," I said. Katy and I headed towards the door.

"Hey, Laura?"

I looked back at Jacob.

"Katy said you're nervous about starting at a new school–"

"Jacob!" Katy glared at him.

I swallowed, unsure whether to be annoyed at Katy or not.

Jacob shrugged. "I was just going to say, Michelle's about your age and she goes to your new school. I could introduce you to her if you wanted? You could teach her how to play Trespassers Club."

I smiled. "Yeah, that'd be cool."

Katy relaxed as I said that. "Thanks," she said to Jacob.

He shrugged again. Katy took my hand as we trudged back through the garden.

CHAPTER FORTY

Katy gave me a boost back up in through my window then tried to climb in herself. She struggled to pull herself up. "Ow! Laura, you'll have to help me." She gripped my arms and I pulled. She just managed to scramble in.

I rubbed my arms when she let go.

"Hey did that hurt?" she asked. "I'm sorry."

"It's okay."

Katy sat down on my bed. "You know I never said how proud I was of you, Munchkin. You did a really good job."

I shrugged.

"No, I mean it. You did much better than me." Katy smiled then she looked down at her hands. "And I'm sorry I told Jacob about you being nervous to start at the new school."

"It's okay."

Katy looked at me. "It's just … I was worried. I mean, you've always hung out with me and I thought you might have a hard time making new friends."

I sighed. "It's fine. Anyway, it'll be cool to meet Jacob's sister."

"Yeah, you can form an all new Trespassers Club." Katy stood up. "Hey, do you think Mum and Dad have noticed we were gone?"

"No, I don't think so. Sounds like they're still watching TV."

"Typical, we're gone for an hour and they don't even care!"

I shrugged. "Well, you do spend a lot of time in your room anyway."

Katy glared at me then laughed. "I guess you're right. Okay, goodnight."

"Katy, can I ask you something?"

"Yeah, sure."

"Is Jacob your boyfriend?"

Katy's eyebrows shot up. "Um …"

"It kind of looked like he was."

"Well, not exactly." Katy had gone pink. "I do like him and if his parents don't ground him for the rest of his life he might be coming around a bit. Is that okay with you?"

"Yeah, Jacob's cool."
Katy smiled. "Night then."
"Yeah goodnight."

CHAPTER FORTY-ONE

The next day Katy went off to help Jacob get ready to go home. I decided to go see Margaret. She was in the garden cleaning the tagging off her house.

"Would you like some help?" I asked.

"Thank you, Laura. There's another sponge in that bucket."

I started scrubbing at the wall.

"Very naughty boys, those two," Margaret said.

I didn't look at her. "Who?" I asked.

"Oh, I think you know." Margaret's eyes twinkled.

I concentrated very hard on squeezing the dirty water out of the sponge.

"It was very clever of you to send me that video," she said.

My eyes widened. "I didn't!"

"It's all right; I'm not going to tell anyone."

I looked at Margaret. She smiled.

"I didn't know what else to do," I said.

"You did the right thing. You and your sister can always come to me for help if you need it." Margaret wiped the last of the tagging off the wall and dropped her sponge back in the bucket. "Now," she said, "why don't you come inside and tell me how it happened."

I smiled. "Well, it all started when Katy and I were playing Trespassers Club …"

ALSO BY HELEN …

THERE'S NO SUCH THING AS HUMANS

Grub is a little monster with a big problem – he's absolutely *terrified* of humans, especially the one his brother says lives under his bed.

Grub's mum says there's no such thing as humans, but even so, they must never go to the edge of the forest. That's fine by Grub, until his brother dares him. He can't refuse a double dare, can he?

Will Grub find humans at the edge of the forest … or something even worse?

DO FRUIT WORRY ABOUT GETTING FAT?

Martin's sister worries about big things, and little things, and everything in between. Martin comes up with a plan to help, but will it stop her worrying?

JENNY NO KNICKERS

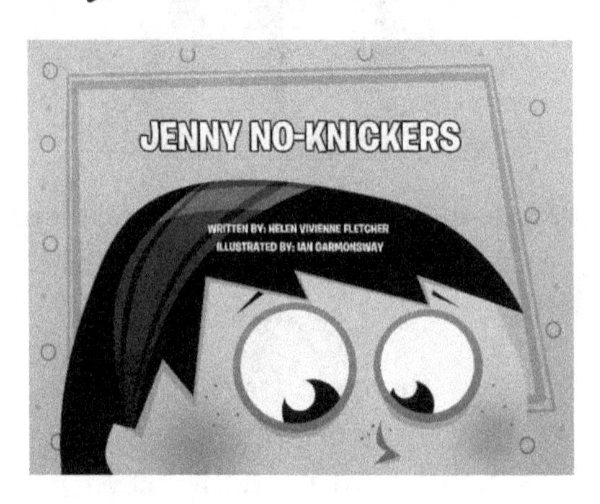

It's washing day at Jenny's house, but oh no! The elastic in all of Jenny's knickers melts in the dryer. How will Jenny solve the no-kickers problem?

AUNT KELLY'S DOG

Davey and Michael can't wait to meet Aunt Kelly's Dog … but what will they do if the dog is a big, scary, people-eating monster?

$1 from the sale of every copy of Aunt Kelly's Dog will be donated to Assistance Dogs New Zealand, to support the work they do in providing dogs to New Zealanders with disabilities.

Find out more about these books at
www.helenvfletcher.com

ACKNOWLEDGEMENTS

A huge thank you to Jess Senior for the fantastic job you did on editing this book, and to Ian and Alana Garmonsway for the beautiful cover. Thanks also to Renata and Ben Spies for encouraging me to finish and publish this story, and for sharing your launch day with me.

Thank you to the people who inspired this book – Amelia who broke into the real abandoned house with me, my mum who told me about the game the neighbourhood kids were playing, and of course those same neighbourhood kids who made up the real Trespassers Club. I've forgotten your names, but I will always remember the times I saw you trespassing in our garden, but pretended I didn't.

ENJOYED THIS BOOK? YOU CAN MAKE A BIG DIFFERENCE.

Reviews are the most powerful tool when it comes to getting attention for my books.

As an indie author, it can be hard to get my books into the hands of readers, but honest reviews of my books help me do just that.

If you've enjoyed this book, I would be very grateful if you could spend just a few minutes leaving a review (it can be as short as you like).

Thank you very much!

ABOUT THE AUTHOR

Helen Vivienne Fletcher has worked in many jobs, doing everything from theatre stage management to phone counselling. She discovered her passion for writing for young people while working as a youth support worker, and now helps children find their own passion for storytelling through her creative writing business, Brain Bunny Workshops.

Helen is the author of numerous books for young people. She has won and been shortlisted for several writing competitions, including making the shortlist for the 2008 Joy Cowley Award, and in 2015 she was named outstanding new playwright at the Wellington Theatre Awards. Helen's poetry and short stories have appeared in various online and print publications, and she regularly performs her spoken word pieces around Wellington. Overall, Helen just loves telling stories, and is always excited when people want to hear or read them.